The Charmed Mystery

Written & Illustrated by Grace Combs

Sophie is staying at Grandma's house for the first time without her mother. She is just a little scared. Her mother gives her a special gift, a locket on a chain, to make her feel less scared. When her grandmother sees it, she seems a little surprised. Sophie loses the necklace and Grandma asks Sophie if she understands why the gift is so special. When Sophie seems puzzled by her question, her grandmother decides that she and Sophie will spend the day not only looking for the missing locket and necklace but also discovering the answer to her question.

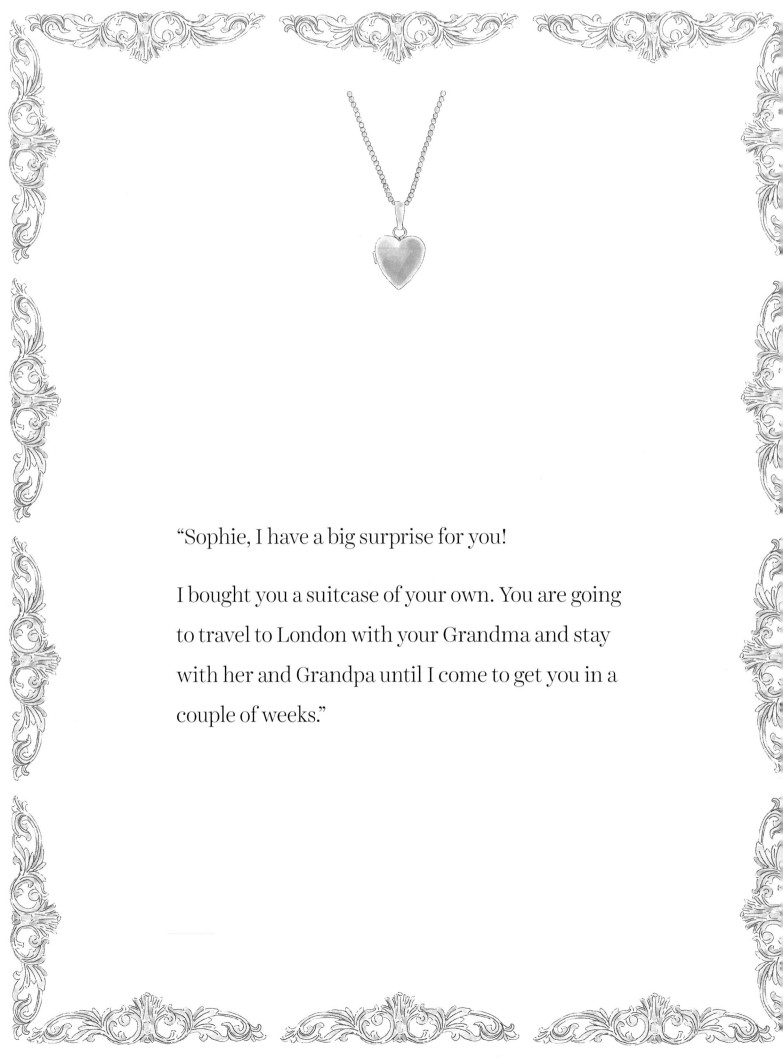

"Sophie, I have a big surprise for you!

I bought you a suitcase of your own. You are going to travel to London with your Grandma and stay with her and Grandpa until I come to get you in a couple of weeks."

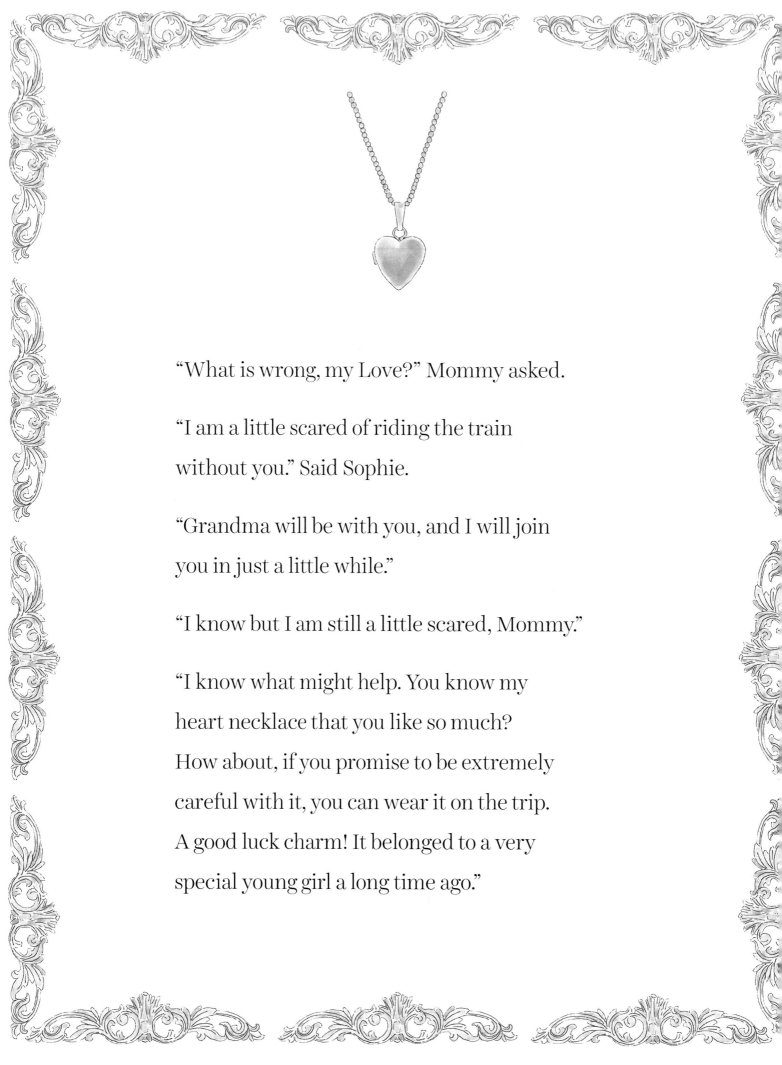

"What is wrong, my Love?" Mommy asked.

"I am a little scared of riding the train without you." Said Sophie.

"Grandma will be with you, and I will join you in just a little while."

"I know but I am still a little scared, Mommy."

"I know what might help. You know my heart necklace that you like so much? How about, if you promise to be extremely careful with it, you can wear it on the trip. A good luck charm! It belonged to a very special young girl a long time ago."

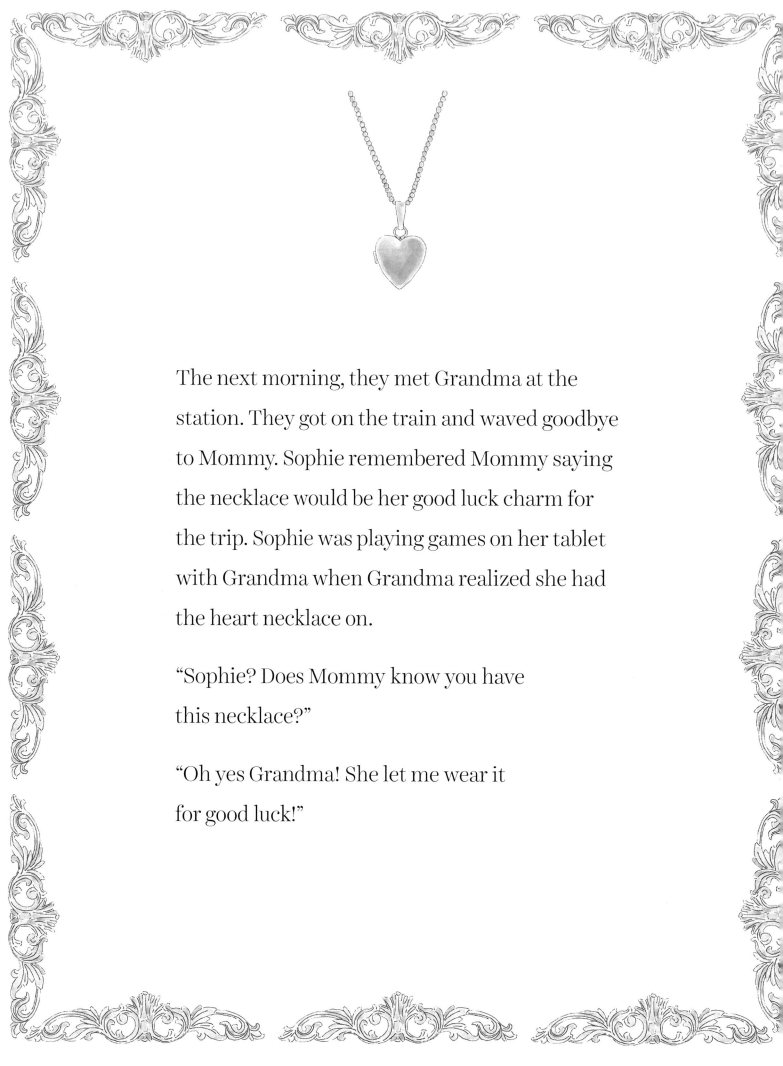

The next morning, they met Grandma at the station. They got on the train and waved goodbye to Mommy. Sophie remembered Mommy saying the necklace would be her good luck charm for the trip. Sophie was playing games on her tablet with Grandma when Grandma realized she had the heart necklace on.

"Sophie? Does Mommy know you have this necklace?"

"Oh yes Grandma! She let me wear it for good luck!"

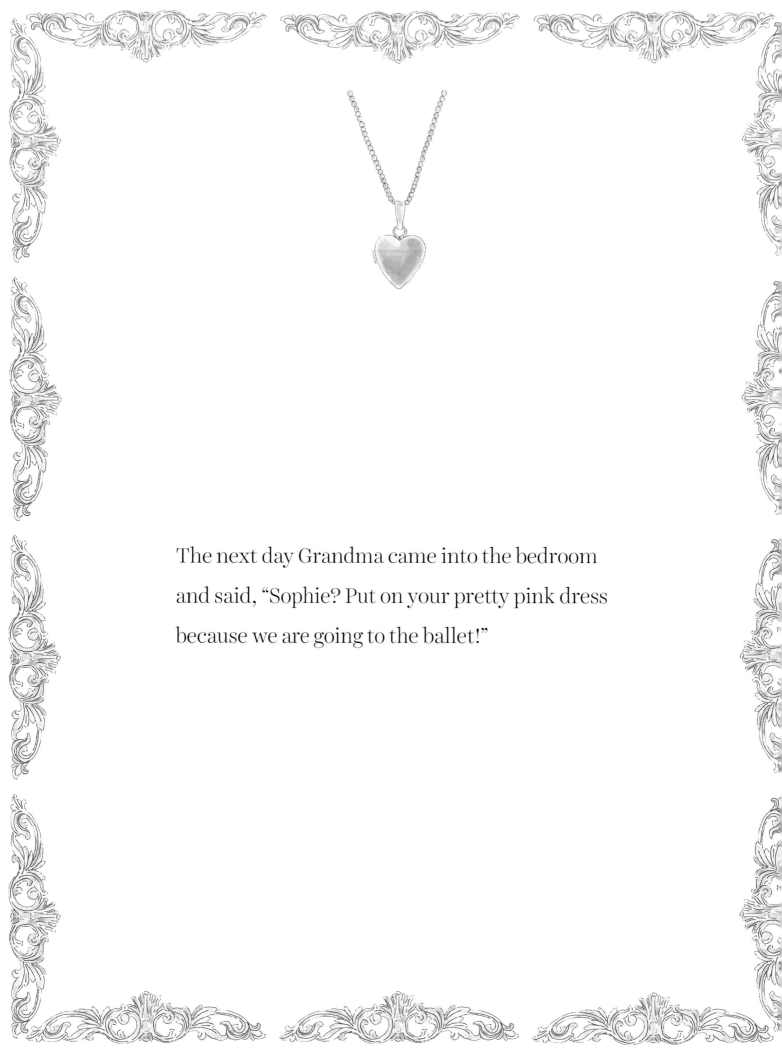

The next day Grandma came into the bedroom and said, "Sophie? Put on your pretty pink dress because we are going to the ballet!"

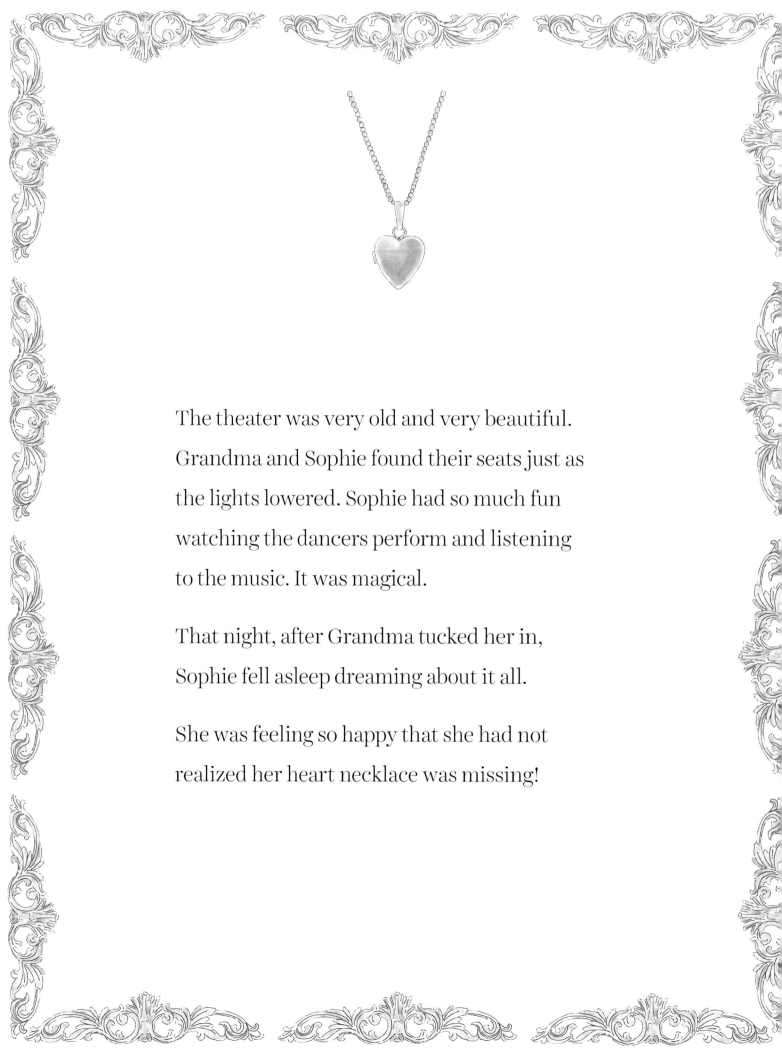

The theater was very old and very beautiful.
Grandma and Sophie found their seats just as
the lights lowered. Sophie had so much fun
watching the dancers perform and listening
to the music. It was magical.

That night, after Grandma tucked her in,
Sophie fell asleep dreaming about it all.

She was feeling so happy that she had not
realized her heart necklace was missing!

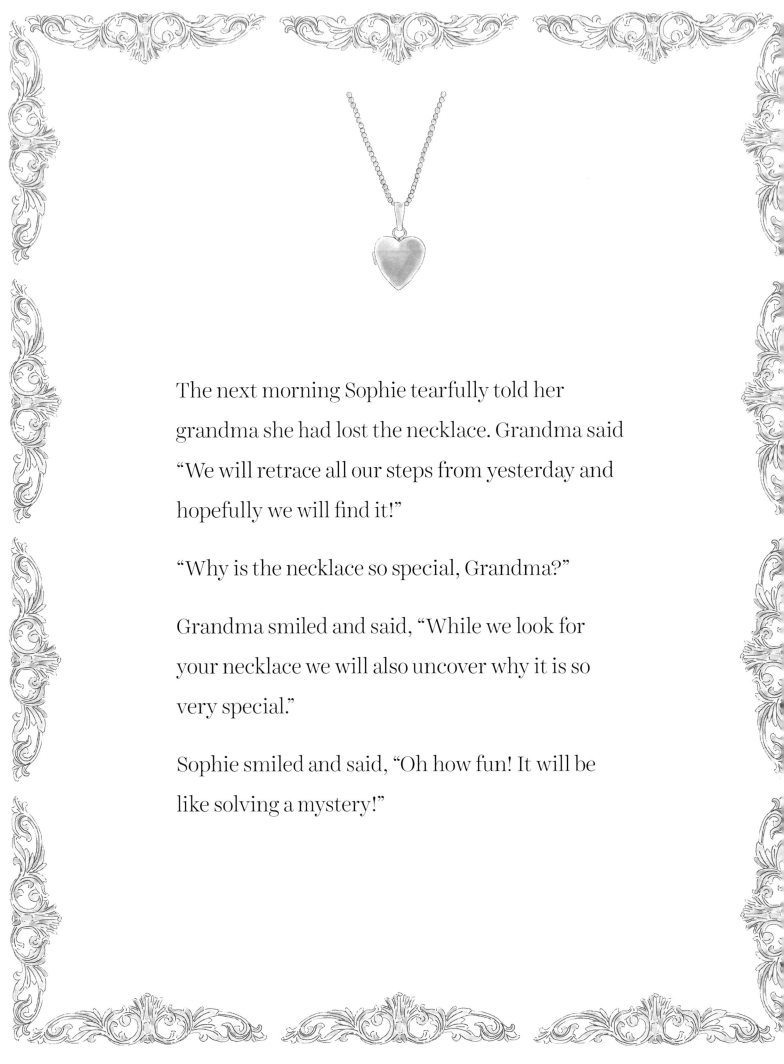

The next morning Sophie tearfully told her grandma she had lost the necklace. Grandma said "We will retrace all our steps from yesterday and hopefully we will find it!"

"Why is the necklace so special, Grandma?"

Grandma smiled and said, "While we look for your necklace we will also uncover why it is so very special."

Sophie smiled and said, "Oh how fun! It will be like solving a mystery!"

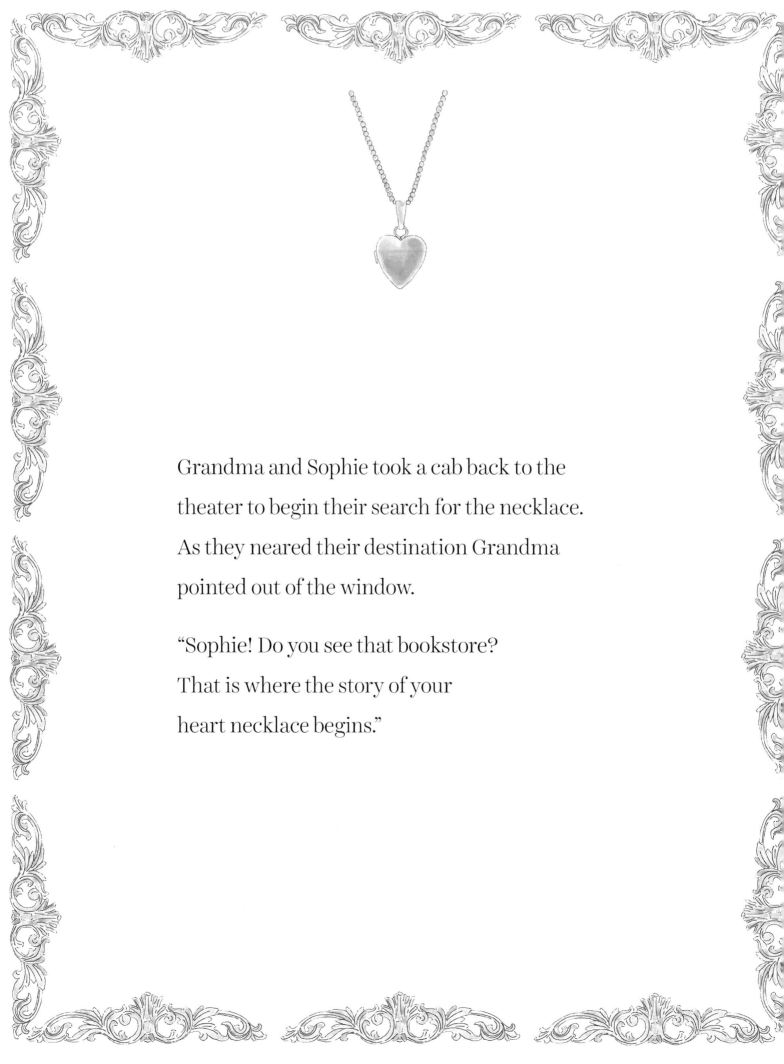

Grandma and Sophie took a cab back to the
theater to begin their search for the necklace.
As they neared their destination Grandma
pointed out of the window.

"Sophie! Do you see that bookstore?
That is where the story of your
heart necklace begins."

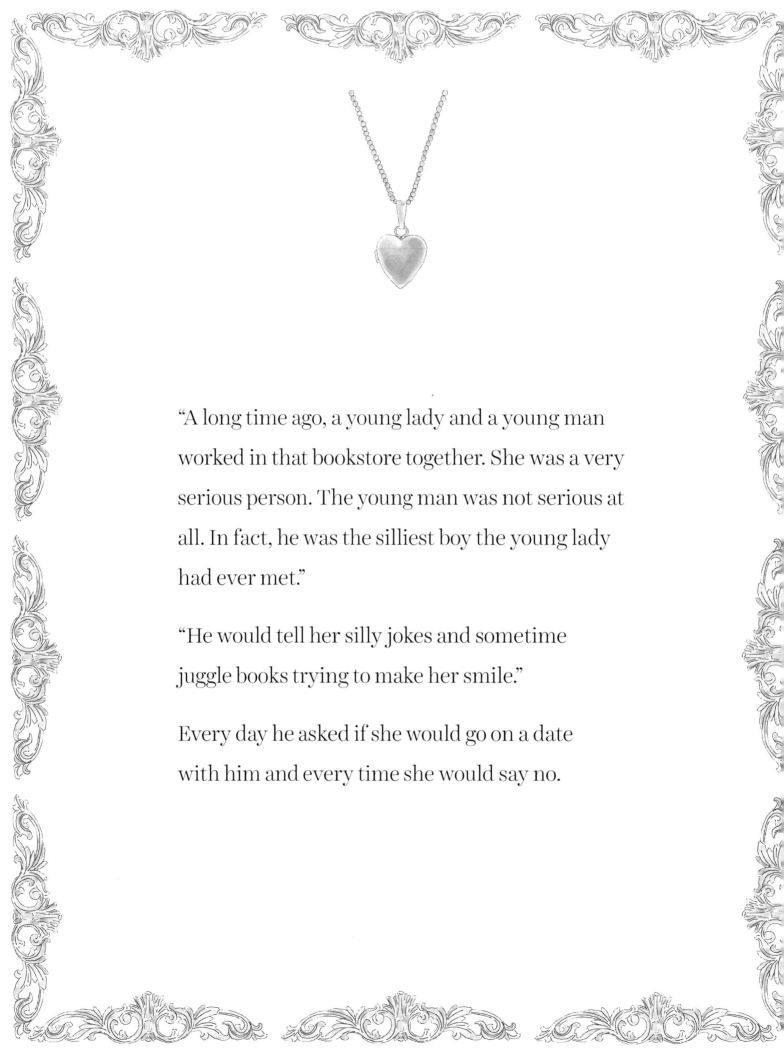

"A long time ago, a young lady and a young man worked in that bookstore together. She was a very serious person. The young man was not serious at all. In fact, he was the silliest boy the young lady had ever met."

"He would tell her silly jokes and sometime juggle books trying to make her smile."

Every day he asked if she would go on a date with him and every time she would say no.

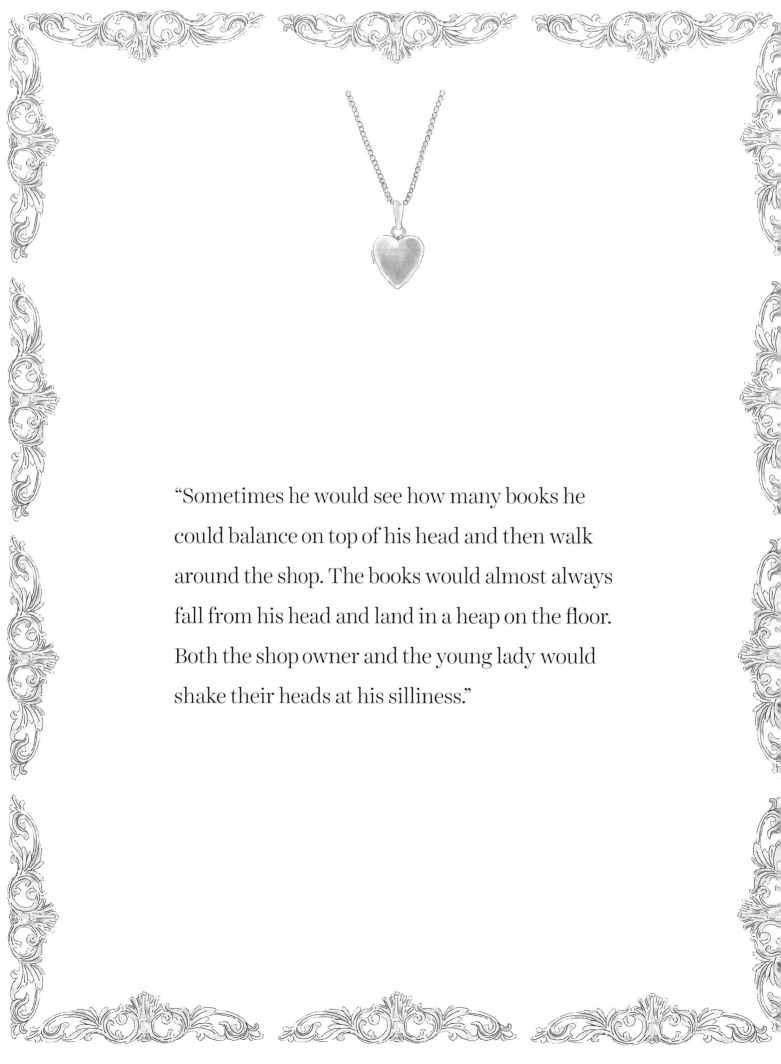

"Sometimes he would see how many books he could balance on top of his head and then walk around the shop. The books would almost always fall from his head and land in a heap on the floor. Both the shop owner and the young lady would shake their heads at his silliness."

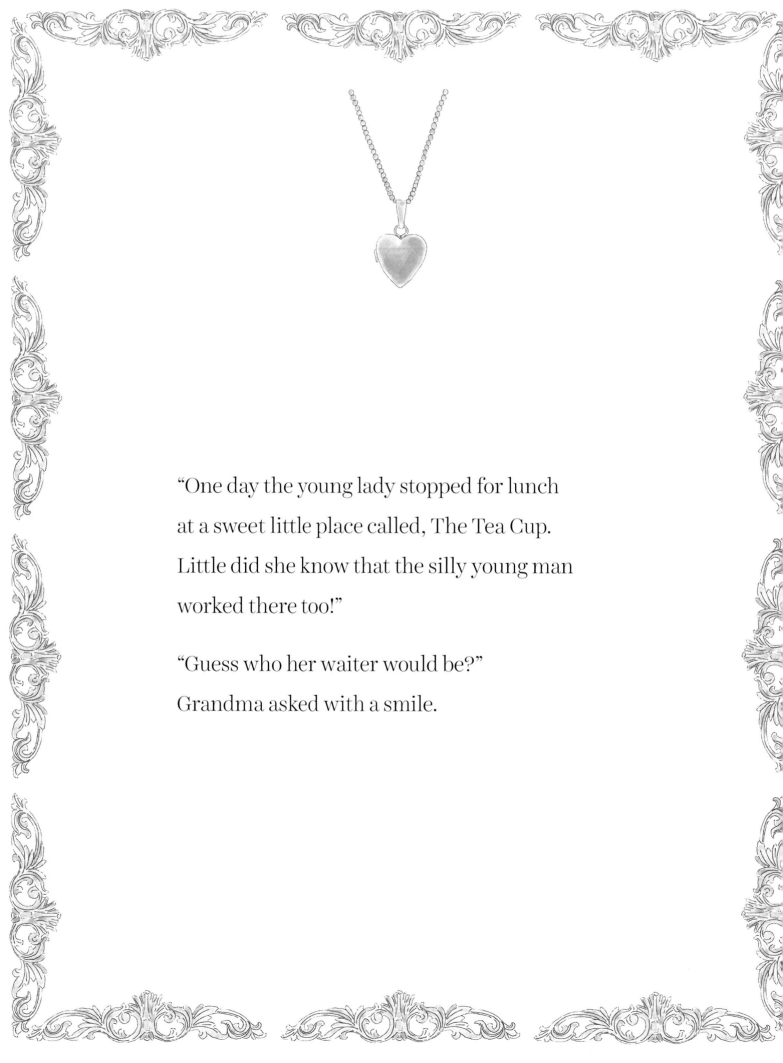

"One day the young lady stopped for lunch
at a sweet little place called, The Tea Cup.
Little did she know that the silly young man
worked there too!"

"Guess who her waiter would be?"
Grandma asked with a smile.

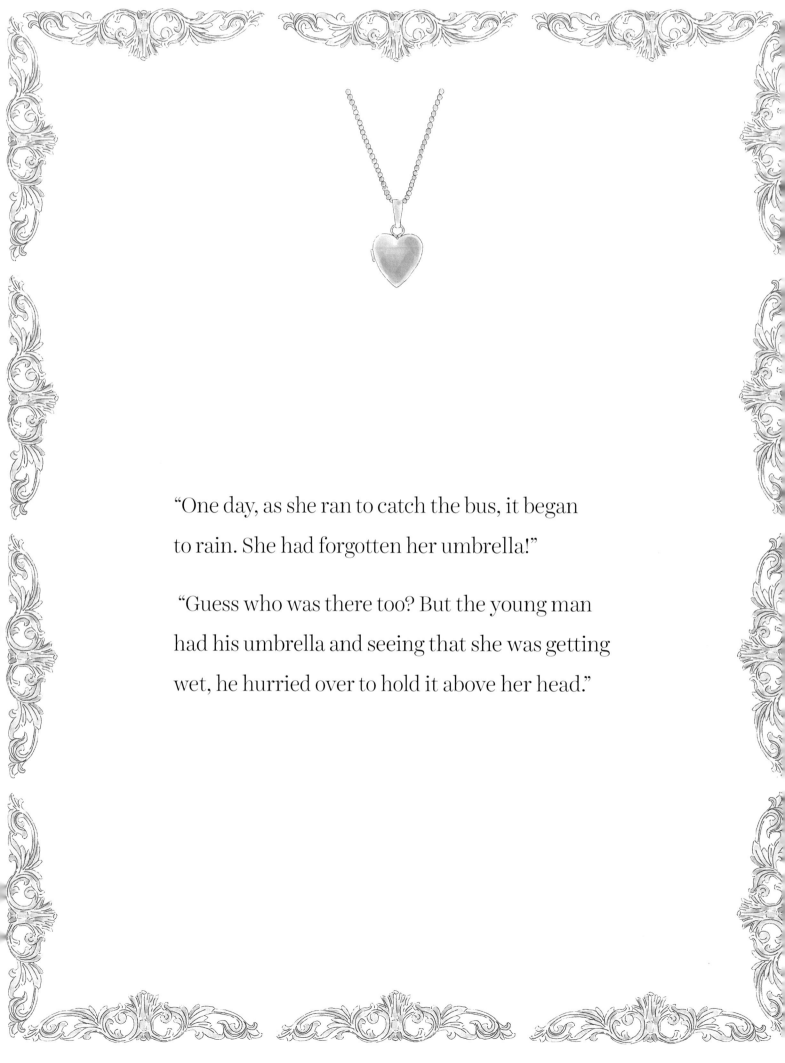

"One day, as she ran to catch the bus, it began to rain. She had forgotten her umbrella!"

"Guess who was there too? But the young man had his umbrella and seeing that she was getting wet, he hurried over to hold it above her head."

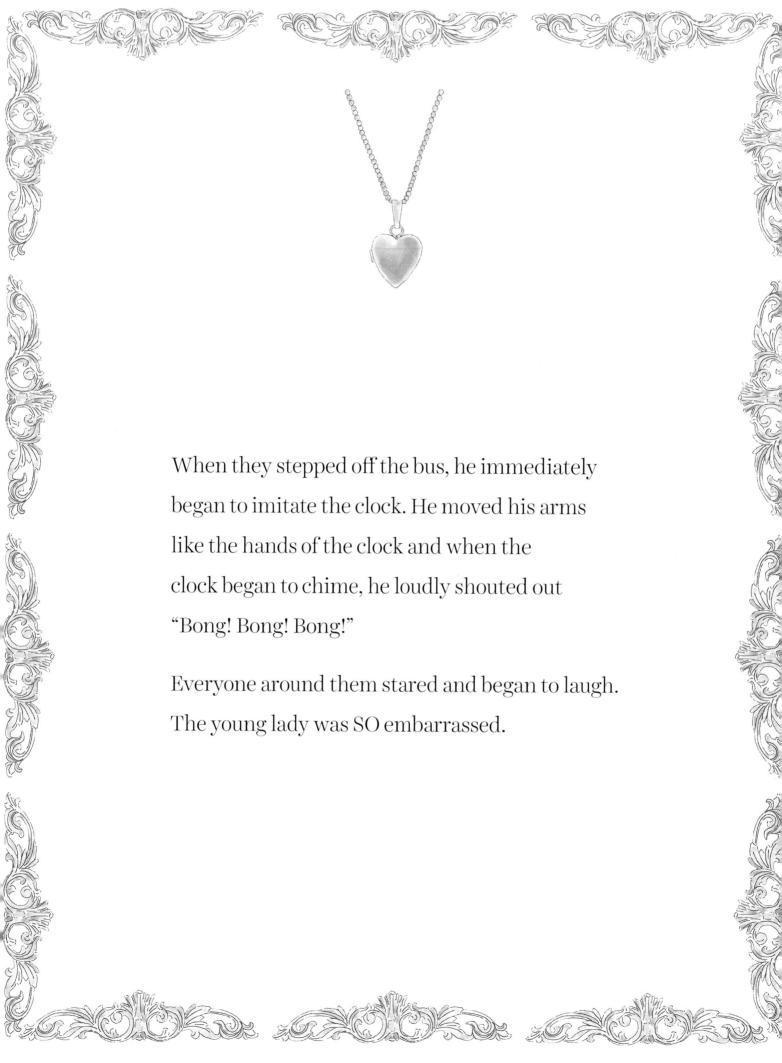

When they stepped off the bus, he immediately
began to imitate the clock. He moved his arms
like the hands of the clock and when the
clock began to chime, he loudly shouted out
"Bong! Bong! Bong!"

Everyone around them stared and began to laugh.
The young lady was SO embarrassed.

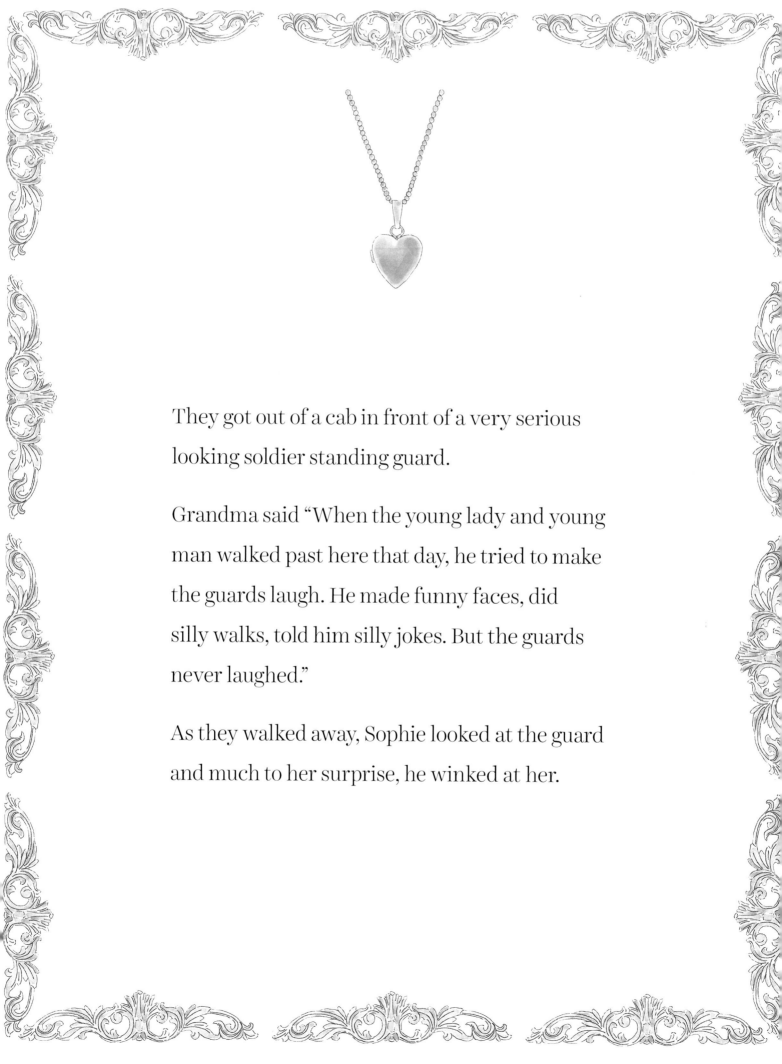

They got out of a cab in front of a very serious looking soldier standing guard.

Grandma said "When the young lady and young man walked past here that day, he tried to make the guards laugh. He made funny faces, did silly walks, told him silly jokes. But the guards never laughed."

As they walked away, Sophie looked at the guard and much to her surprise, he winked at her.

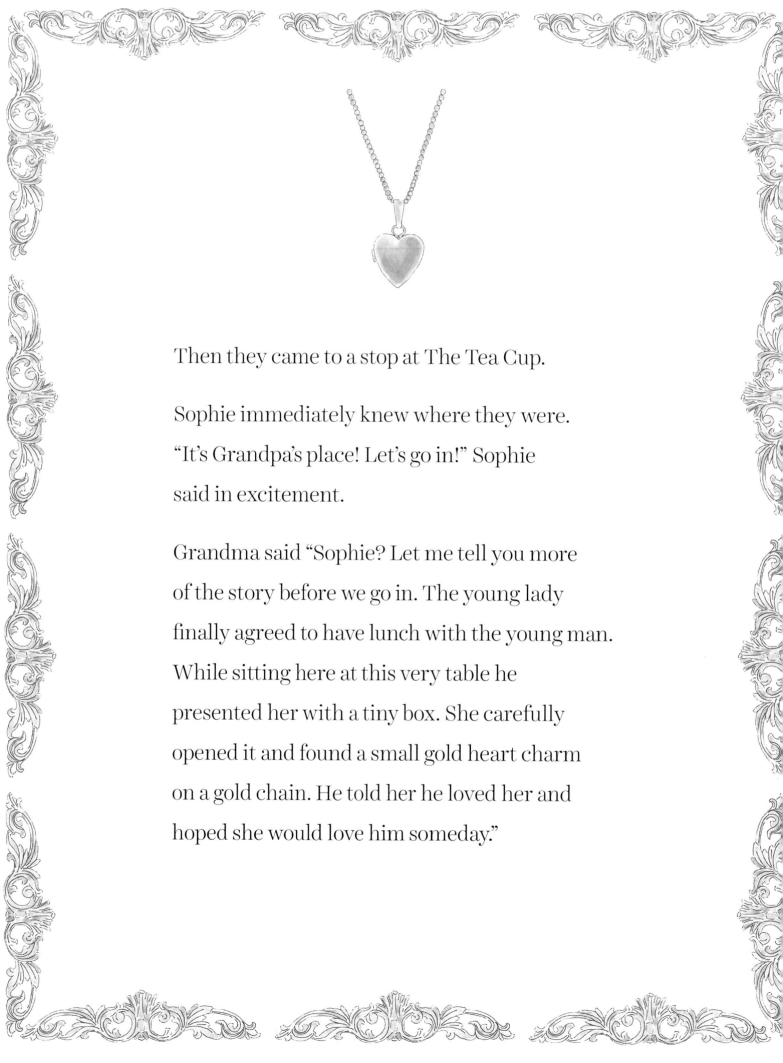

Then they came to a stop at The Tea Cup.

Sophie immediately knew where they were. "It's Grandpa's place! Let's go in!" Sophie said in excitement.

Grandma said "Sophie? Let me tell you more of the story before we go in. The young lady finally agreed to have lunch with the young man. While sitting here at this very table he presented her with a tiny box. She carefully opened it and found a small gold heart charm on a gold chain. He told her he loved her and hoped she would love him someday."

The Tea Cup

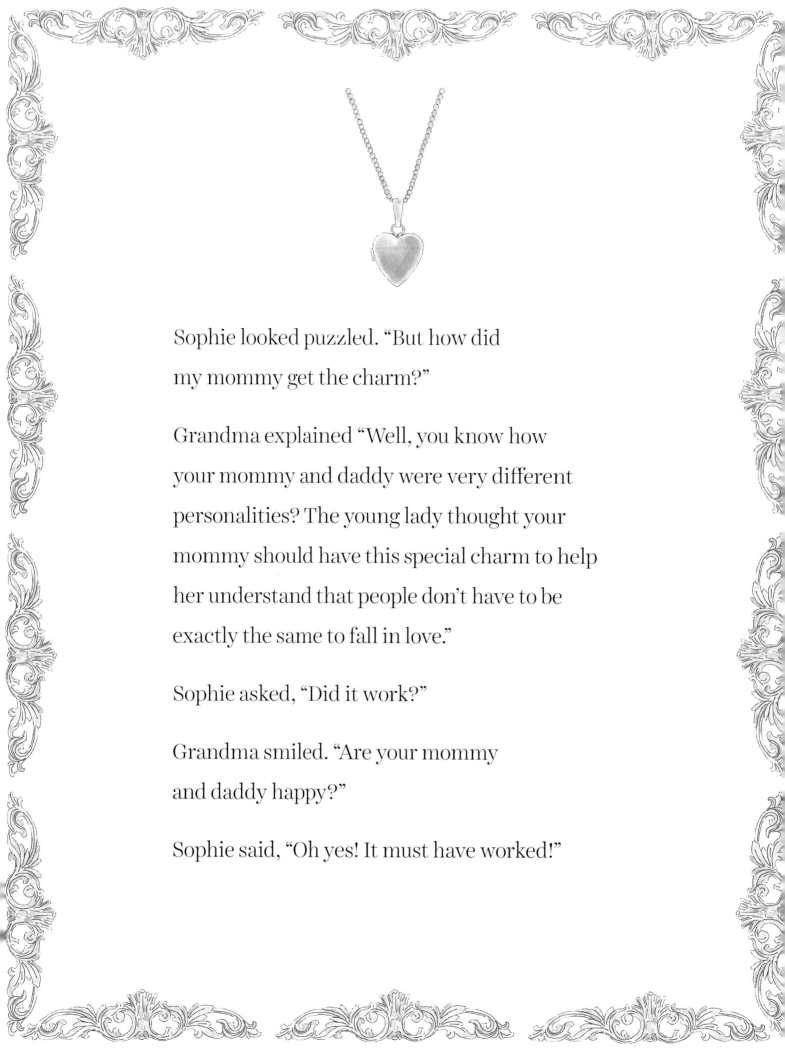

Sophie looked puzzled. "But how did my mommy get the charm?"

Grandma explained "Well, you know how your mommy and daddy were very different personalities? The young lady thought your mommy should have this special charm to help her understand that people don't have to be exactly the same to fall in love."

Sophie asked, "Did it work?"

Grandma smiled. "Are your mommy and daddy happy?"

Sophie said, "Oh yes! It must have worked!"

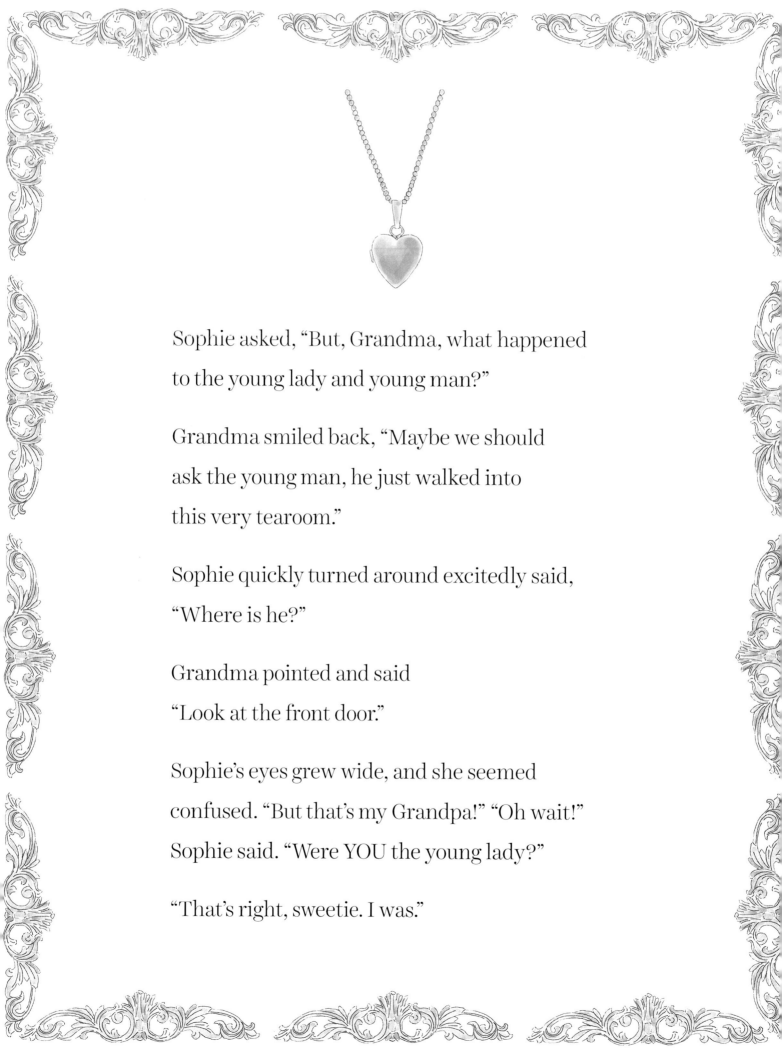

Sophie asked, "But, Grandma, what happened to the young lady and young man?"

Grandma smiled back, "Maybe we should ask the young man, he just walked into this very tearoom."

Sophie quickly turned around excitedly said, "Where is he?"

Grandma pointed and said "Look at the front door."

Sophie's eyes grew wide, and she seemed confused. "But that's my Grandpa!" "Oh wait!" Sophie said. "Were YOU the young lady?"

"That's right, sweetie. I was."

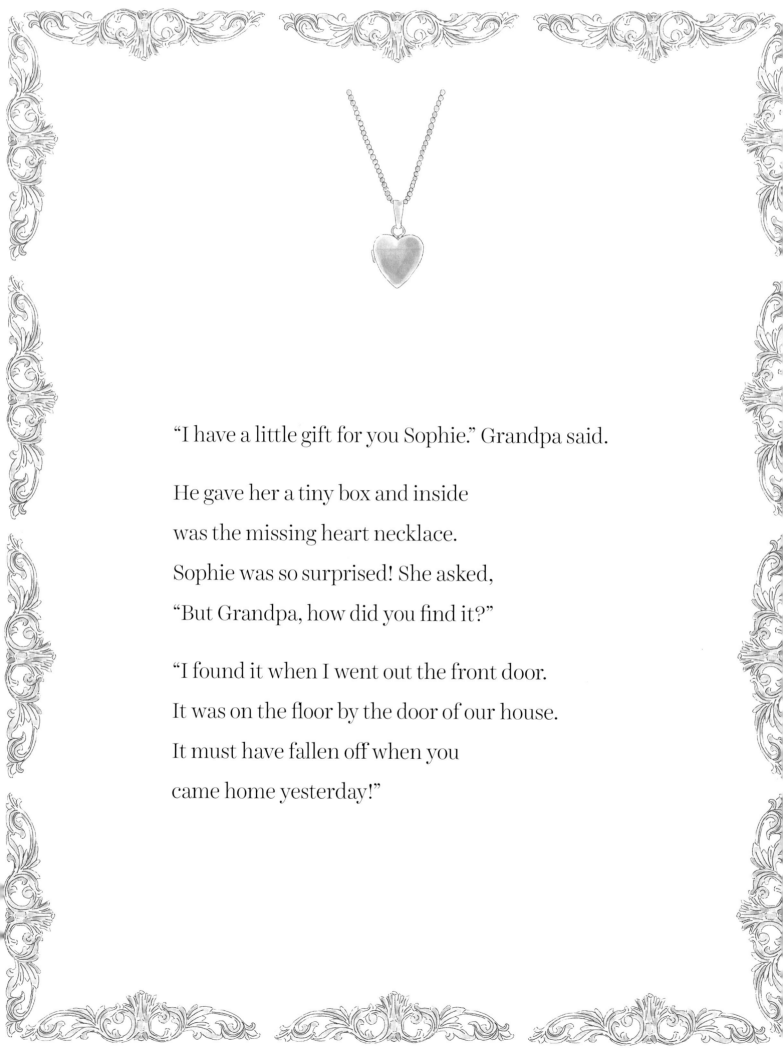

"I have a little gift for you Sophie." Grandpa said.

He gave her a tiny box and inside

was the missing heart necklace.

Sophie was so surprised! She asked,

"But Grandpa, how did you find it?"

"I found it when I went out the front door.

It was on the floor by the door of our house.

It must have fallen off when you

came home yesterday!"

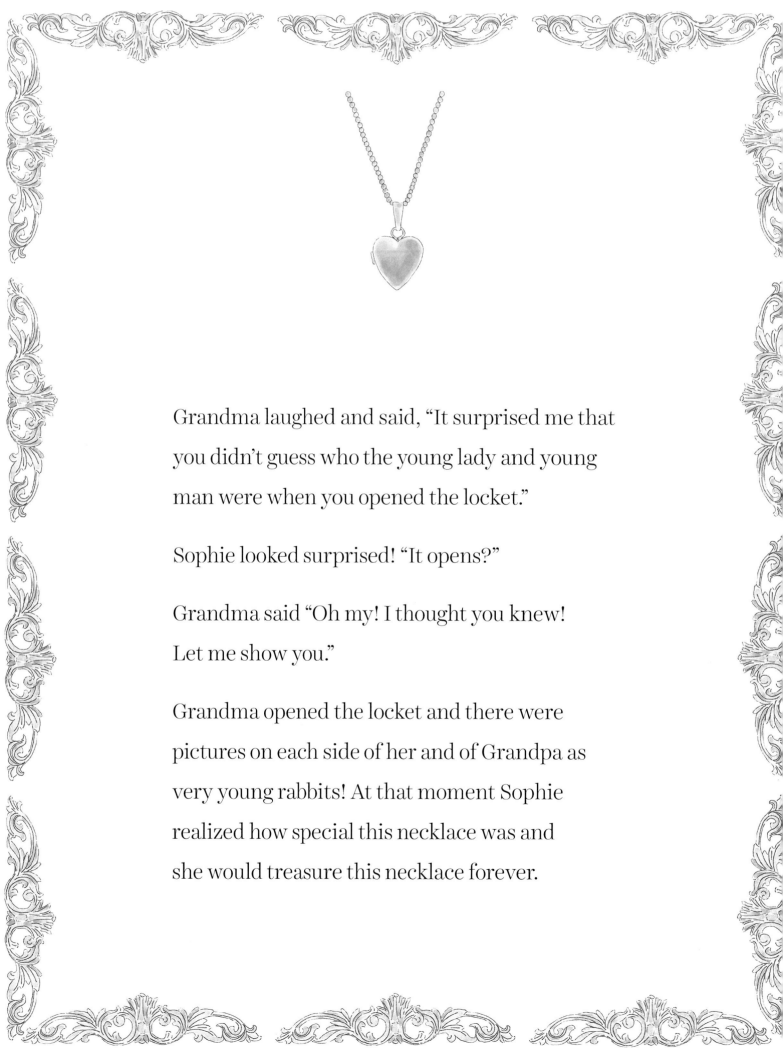

Grandma laughed and said, "It surprised me that you didn't guess who the young lady and young man were when you opened the locket."

Sophie looked surprised! "It opens?"

Grandma said "Oh my! I thought you knew! Let me show you."

Grandma opened the locket and there were pictures on each side of her and of Grandpa as very young rabbits! At that moment Sophie realized how special this necklace was and she would treasure this necklace forever.

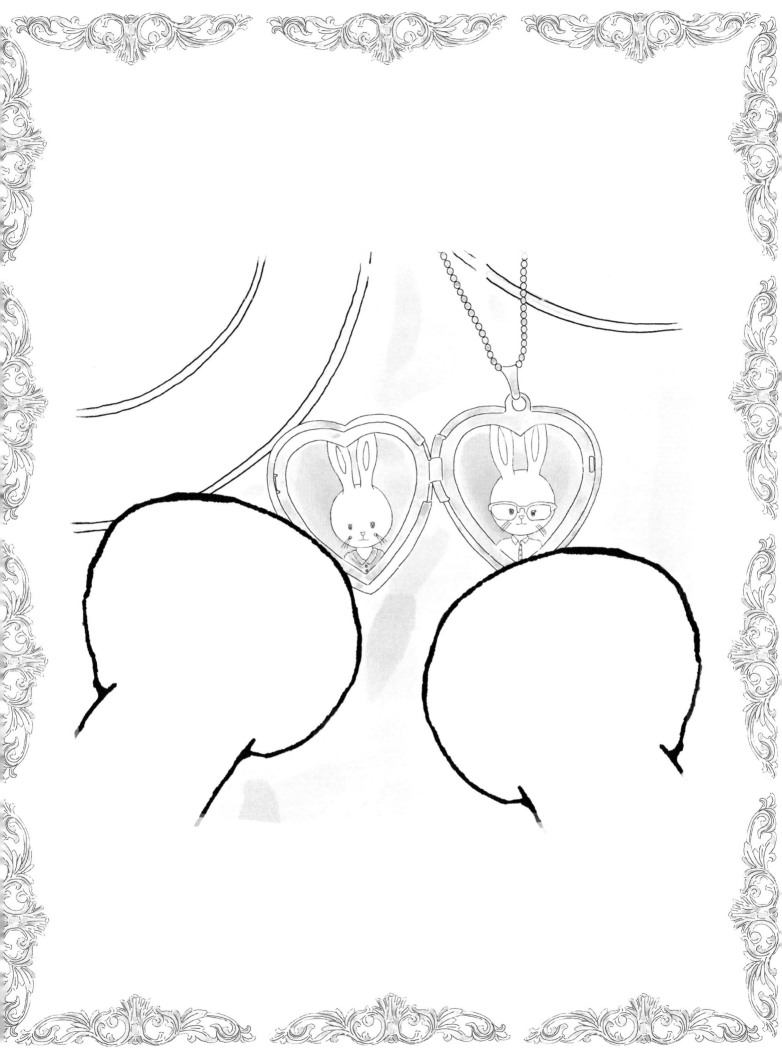

Author and Illustrator

Grace Combs

Graduated from Columbus College of Art and Design
in 2021 with a Bachelor Degree in Illustration.

Made in United States
North Haven, CT
05 October 2023

42394869R00027